OUR OWN LITTLE FICTIONS

Stories from the Road

By Ron Rhody

Outer Banks Publishing Group
Raleigh/Outer Banks

FIRST EDITION – November 2018

ISBN 13 – 978-1-7320452-1-7
ISBN 10 – 1-7320452-1-6
eISBN - 978-1-3102013-1-8

"If we don't tell each other our stories, how will we know what life is all about?"

For Miss South and Lucy Jane Craycraft and Cecil Webster.

And Ken Hart and Harry Towles.

And Donnie.

Thanks is too weak a word.

The Old Capitol

I

TO BEGIN

This is not a memoir.

I would not presume to try to write a memoir.

Memoirs are the province of people who are famous, or notorious, or otherwise of note.

My wife has informed me that I am none of the these.

So this is a story instead.

What Woody thought emboldens me—Woody Guthrie, that master teller of tales and singer of songs.

Stories are what tie us all together. They're how we connect with each other.

Each life is a story. Each is unique. Each has in it moments that can move us and teach us and strengthen us and comfort us.

Stories are our markers. If they're not told and passed on, they're lost forever.

If we don't tell each other our stories, how will we know what life is all about?

Country Boy

I haven't decided whether I was just a poor country boy trying to do the best he could in a world he never made ... or a poet and a lover.

I prefer to think the latter, but ...

When I say country boy, think of Kentucky, think of the Bluegrass of Kentucky.

Think of a land where, in the spring, broad meadows of blue-tipped grass flow in gentle swells across the countryside like waves on a peaceful sea. Think of small creeks gurgling over polished pebbles and white plank fences lining pastures where young colts play. Think of cornfields in rich river bottoms and tobacco, golden brown, hanging in racks in big white barns whose sides are open to the season to let the sun and wind do its work.

And moonlight.

Lord, there is no light so soft and bright as the light of a full moon on a summer's night with the whippoorwills calling and the big bass moving up on the rocky points at Lake Cumberland.

Think of that.

I haven't mentioned the snow-clad hills of winter, or the bright woods of spring with the dogwoods and the redbuds blooming. I haven't mentioned how he died on his feet arguing that blacks had rights. I haven't mentioned the visitors at Romance, or what we did about the cyanide in the river, or the

L.A. riots, or the Tech Center rapist, or my time among the godlike creatures in the big black tower at the foot of Nob Hill.

Or even the day they killed the King and brought the old King back.

I am basing most of this on memory, but I will try to make it true. Though there is the lesson of Rashomon to be remembered, and the fact that truth, like beauty, may lie in the eye of the beholder—for, after all, we all live in our own little fictions, don't we?

As for the lover and poet part, think of John Donne and Andrew Marvell. Think of King Solomon's Song of Songs and the Rubaiyat. Think of the real Thomas Wolfe searching down that lost lane end into heaven, looking for a stone, a leaf, an unfound door.

Think of your first serious kiss. Think of the morning coming and the scent of her still warm and fragrant on the pillow. Think of music on summer nights drifting down the hill to the sandy beach by the river. And sunsets hanging on as long as they can over Hanalei Bay. And how peaceful it is.

Think of that, country boy, think of that.

Frankfort from the Daniel Boone Monument overlook

Okay. That should set the stage, should give you a rough idea of what to expect.

That said, we'll start the story at a time I particularly remember in early childhood. I was about four or five. I don't recall much before then.

From there we'll take off for the strange and distant places I found myself in while still a boy, but get back in time for growing up.

So, pretend it's summer, almost dark. We've been swimming and now we're sitting around a campfire on the little beach on the river below Big Eddy getting warm. No moon. Lots of stars. A whippoorwill calling somewhere off in the distance. A breeze sneaking through the trees. The faint sound of water lapping against the shore.

Peaceful.

Pretend we're talking. Pretend you're listening to me. Not reading, listening.

Pretend you're listening.

Home Places

My mother was afraid of thunderstorms at night.

We lived a long block away from the newspaper where my father worked as a young reporter. The quickest way there was across the railroad tracks and up a dimly lit alley that ran behind the Newberry Five & Dime and the Grand Theatre.

Our apartment was on the second floor of a big brick house on the corner of Broadway and Madison across from the Old Capitol.

Madison is gone now, a casualty of the zeal of urban renewal. In its day, it was a stately street. Legislators lived there. The house where the Beauchamp–Sharp tragedy occurred was just down the block.

In the earliest days, the grounds on which the Capitol stands had been the town square. The grounds cover four city blocks, and people were always there—young mothers wheeling baby carriages, small children running and playing, men sitting quietly on benches in the shade reading their papers or talking.

The place was a like a private park for me.

In the summer, it was shady and cool, and I could run unfettered among the trees and over the rises, and in the fall, when the oaks and the maples dropped their leaves, I could kick happily through the mounds of red and orange the groundsmen had raked up.

The square is on the northern edge of the downtown business district. It was bounded on three sides by residential streets such as the one we lived on, and in front by Broadway, the main street of the town. Railroad tracks ran down the center of Broadway and all traffic stopped while the trains passed through.

To the rear of the square is Fort Hill. Yankee cannon had been entrenched there when John Hunt Morgan's Confederate raiders briefly threatened the town before the battle at Perryville—the one the Yankees won. Lincoln had said before the fight, "I hope to have God on my side, but I must have Kentucky."

The Old Capitol building commands the center of the square. It is made from Kentucky River marble and fashioned after an ancient Greek temple.

The only Kentucky Governor ever killed in office was shot on the walk leading up to it—William Goebel. This almost triggered a civil war. Politics is passionate business in the Commonwealth. A brass plate marks the place where he fell.

Later, after we had moved to another part of town and I had grown old enough to be allowed out after dinner to play, we'd chase each other among the trees near that marker and tell stories of old Goebel's ghost walking these grounds while the whole town slept.

So there we were, my mother and I, in that second-floor apartment, she just barely into her twenties, enormously proud when my father's byline appeared in the morning paper, but apprehensive at being left alone with only me at night while he did the work that newspapermen do.

She managed fine—except for thunderstorms at night.

When the tempests of spring came roaring down the valley, whipping the trees across the street into a frenzy, thunder cracking like cannons, she would grab me, no matter the hour, throw her coat around us both and run with me in her arms through the wind and the rain up the alley to the *Journal* and the safety of my father.

I do not know what they must have thought of us, charging drenched and breathless into the newsroom. The *Journal* was a morning newspaper. The editor and reporters, unless out on assignment, had to be at work on their stories for the next morning's paper. She was so young and pretty, they must have smiled and felt protective. They were Kentuckians. Kentuckians are honor bound to be gallant and chivalrous to damsels in distress.

I do know that after we'd dried off, my father would take me, frightened by my mother's fear and our dash through the storm, and stand me on the work table in front of the big window that looked out on the street and he would stand behind me with his arms around me and we would watch the storm. We'd watch how the wind danced with the trees and count the seconds from the flash of the lightning to the crack of the thunder.

He'd tell me that all that the wind and rain, all that thunder and the lightning—it was magic, a magic show nature had arranged just for us—a thing to wonder at and enjoy. Not something to be afraid of.

Afterward, when the storm had passed, he would walk us back through the alley to home and see us safely settled.

My mother never fully overcame her fear, but after a while the fear shrank to mere uneasiness and we did not run through the alley anymore.

Ever after, I have loved wild thunderstorms at night.

Madison Street isn't there anymore, but I see it still.

The town I grew up in isn't there anymore, either. Oh, there is a town there. A fine town. Just not the one I grew up in.

I still see that one, though, superimposed in my mind over the look and the feel of the town as it is now.

I bring the matter up here at the beginning because I think home places, the places where we are born and grow up, I think they mold and shape us. They set our sense of self, our manners, the ease and confidence we hold, the way we talk, the way we think.

The look and the feel of them comfort us and reassure us.

And the people who are their hearts, and the values they embrace and the acts they perform, and the expectations of us they hold, as we are growing up, these things have a fundamental influence on who we are and what we become.

I liked that little town a lot.

But we left.

I don't remember exactly how old I was—ten, maybe eleven. I remember I was beginning to work on my Scout merit badges.

Our wanderings took us out to California—to Yreka up in the mountains near the Oregon border where my father went to edit the *Siskiyou Daily News*. At one time Yreka had been a boomtown, "the richest square mile on earth"—until the gold ran out.

By the time we arrived, it had morphed into a hub for the ranching and timbering operations of that part of the state, and the county seat.

Yreka and its mountains were a great change from the rolling meadows of the Bluegrass. The views, my god, the views—out across high meadows rimmed by granite peaks, some still snow-clad even in summer, and skies at night so clear that the stars seemed close enough to reach up and pluck.

And the fish were different. These had rainbows on their sides and they finned in the current of the McCloud in ice-cold water from the snowmelt off Mount Shasta.

I could have been very satisfied there. We all could have been. My little sister Ann and little brother Donnie liked it, and Mom pulled the place around her like a warm comforter.

But the bug bit again, and after a while we packed up and moved all the way back across the country ... to Sarasota, on the west coast of Florida where the Ringling Bros. and Barnum & Bailey Circus had its winter headquarters and where a bigger newspaper awaited my father. This time, Mary Lou, who had just been born, was with us.

At Sarasota, we lived way out of town in a house with a tin roof that sat on cinderblocks, back a sandy lane among pine trees and palmettos. At night, the sound of pine needles falling on the roof sometimes sounded like a gentle rain. The ocean was just a short hike further along.

Howard Henderson, a good friend of my dad's and a well-known columnist for the Louisville *Courier-Journal,* Kentucky's largest newspaper, came to live with us for a while when we were there, to recover from an illness. Ann and Donnie were his companions. While Dad was at work, they'd walk with Mr. Henderson down to a brackish pond near the end of the lane and keep him company while he fished.

There were no fish there that anyone knew of, but Mr. Henderson didn't care. He was up and about and not in pain and the sun was shining. He fished off a rickety old dock, sitting on a raggedy canvas stool, using a long cane pole and a red and white bobber. If a fish happened by, that would be nice, thank you kindly, but not at all necessary.

I rode a Greyhound bus into town for school, catching it where our lane ran into the blacktop of the Tamiami Trail, the main road from Tampa across to Miami.

Florida was flat as a skillet, all palm trees and pines and white sandy beaches. No grass around anywhere. No hills. Enormous sunsets, though.

It was new enough and different enough that it kept our interest and we were getting adjusted and beginning to understand the place when the editor's job at the *Dothan Eagle* in Alabama opened up. So there we went.

Same drill. We stayed a while, were just settling in, when my father decided to move again—this time full circle, back to Frankfort.

By then it was time for me to start high school.

All that moving, all that being dropped into unfamiliar towns and ushered into strange schools where all the little cliques are already set and you know no one and no one knows you or has reason to care—all that meant you had to figure out fairly rapidly how to carve your place among strangers. And hold tight to the people you knew you could count on … your mom and dad and your brother and sister.

It was good to be home again.

Pete's Corner

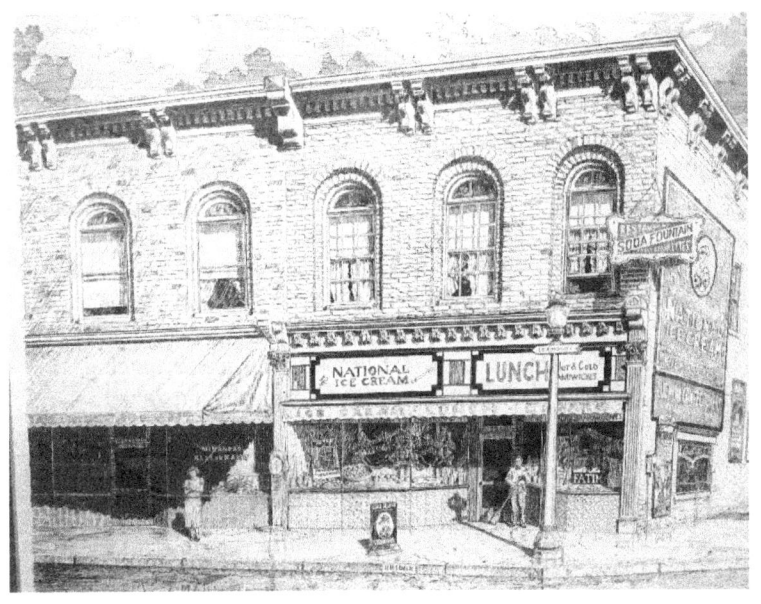

Now I'm going to jump ahead.

I'm not trying to lay this story out chronologically.

What I want to do, with alacrity so as not to bore you, is get us from where we began to where we'll be when I'm on my way to becoming whatever I'll become.

But bear with me, for as I pull all this together, one matter may suggest another and I may get distracted and may momentarily stray off course.

I may even repeat myself because I am remembering, and you understand how that is, how one memory triggers another.

It will all come together in time.

If You Want to Play

It's a soft spring night on Pete's Corner with a slight breeze running up from the river and ruffling the trees behind us. A car stops occasionally for the stoplight.

Several of the guys are horsing around under the lamppost. Monk and I have walked across the street to take a seat on the wall and continue the conversation we'd begun over coffee inside and that will continue into the night as others join us. We're working over the problems that have so far stymied the world's great thinkers. We're sixteen, in our junior year in high school. We had the answers.

Monk later became Charles M. Hudson, Jr., PhD., distinguished scholar, renowned authority on the native peoples of the American Southeast, and a chaired professor in the Department of Anthropology at the University of Georgia. He was probably the smartest among us, definitely the toughest, and hands-down the most indomitable. The story about that comes later.

The night I'm talking about now was the night before spring football practice was to begin.

I had lettered as a sophomore and again as a junior, starting at linebacker on defense. We played both ways then, offense and defense. Next year, our year, our senior year, I'd start both ways. That was golden. That was great. I could hardly wait.

Football was a large part of our lives then—had been since we were in grade school. We started out playing choose-up games on playgrounds and in backyards, no pads, tackle, and worked up to regular weekend contests with set teams, still playing tackle and still without armor. Other than an occasional skinned knee or bloody nose, no one got hurt that I can remember.

When we moved up to high school, many of us had been playing together for years. We got to run around on grassy fields knocking each other down—laughing, teasing, testing who was faster or tougher, or too stubborn to stay down. It was exciting and demanding. It was the best play ever. And it taught us things we would never have learned so thoroughly in any other way.

We learned that going half-speed is a sure way to lose.

We learned that blocking and tackling is what wins ball games, not fancy footwork and dancing around.

We learned you can't make a touchdown all by yourself.

But the most important, for me at least, was Leo's lesson.

Leo Yarutis was our head coach at Georgetown, the one in Kentucky, not the one in D.C. Leo had been an All-Southeastern Conference guard at the University of Kentucky under Bear Bryant in the years when Kentucky was a football powerhouse as well as a basketball powerhouse. The weak or the timid didn't play for Bryant or make All-SEC guard.

Leo was working on his doctorate in psychology while coaching at Georgetown College. Leo could run through brick walls, leap tall buildings in a single bound, and walk on water if any was in the way. If Leo said it, we believed it. If Leo said do it, we did it.

In the last practice before our opening game, a freshman quarterback taking snaps got blindsided by a 240-pound tackle.

In those days we didn't wear facemasks. The quarterback, a tall, slim kid from somewhere in West Kentucky, had taken an elbow across the mouth and lay dazed and bleeding on the grass. We all gathered round. His mouth was smashed. He was gagging as he tried to breathe through the blood.

Leo walked over, looked down, looked up at all of us standing there watching, looked back down at the boy and said to him, not unkindly, as if explaining something, "It's a rough game, son. If you want to play, you gotta suck it up and go."

Leo turned then and walked away to get the huddle formed for the next play.

Still dazed, the kid struggled up, blood dripping down his face, and limped slowly off the field.

If you want to play, you gotta suck it up and go.

Pete's Corner was an institution.

The town's softball field was just across the street. Softball was a big deal at the time. The town's factories and stores all fielded teams. They competed heatedly.

Just up the block was the YMCA. There was a gym there and a ping-pong table and an indoor swimming pool. There was always a lot of activity around.

Our school didn't have a lunchroom. So it was either bring your lunch, walk home for lunch, or take the two-block stroll down to Pete's for the famous chili.

After school, most stopped by for a Coke or coffee or just to lean against the corner lamppost and watch the girls go by. After supper, if it was still early enough, you went to Pete's. You knew somebody would be there. You'd find a booth inside and sit and talk. Or you'd move outside to stand around under the lamppost telling stories, or cross the street to sit on the wall above the softball field and wait to see what might happen, as Monk and I were doing that night.

Soon enough, someone would start a song.

There was a lot of singing in my family.

My mother sang to us at night when we were young—lullabies to go to sleep by, my father, too, if he was there. He wasn't there often at night. The *Journal* was a morning newspaper. The reporters and editors worked at night.

I was a boy soprano and was herded into the church choir for Sunday morning services as a six year old. When my voice changed to bass, I stayed with it through high school and on to the chapel choir in college.

The first time I was exposed to harmony was with my father.

I must have been five or so, a Saturday morning in the back of a car going somewhere to fish. He was up front with whomever we were going with and they were singing. I knew the tune and joined in. He turned around and began to sing with me. Only it wasn't the tune I was singing. It was something else, something that made what I was singing sound better, something different, but good.

I stopped. Frowned.

"That's not the way it goes," I said.

"It's harmony," he said. "Try another one."

So I started on another and he started singing with me—not the melody I sang, but his own. As his voice blended with mine and our two melodies ran along arm in arm, they made a sound so rich and right I stopped again in wonder.

"Harmony," he said again, smiling. "You'll learn it soon."

One night, in an old hotel near Bridgend, a small village not far from Cardiff in Wales, a cold, sleety night, with a Welsh friend I worked with, in the bar there after dinner, peat fire burning, lights low and mellow, the room full of Welshmen taking me for an Englishman for whom they have no fondness, someone started a song.

I listened. The Welsh are such marvelous singers I hadn't the effrontery to try to join in, but my friend did and he nudged me to join as well.

There were a few frowns at first, but as I began to find the notes and make the harmony, and my accent was heard, things loosened.

"Buy you a drink, Yank?"

"Only if the next one's on me."

The fire burned down and the night ran out as we sat there singing.

I became an honorary Welshman that night.

It might have been the single malt, but I think it was the harmony.

Most of the boys in my class sang—not well, but earnestly.

Miss South saw to that.

Miss Eudora L. South, our music teacher. Miss South was small, cherubic, dedicated, and determined.

You were to love music. You were to experience the joy of making it.

She got us in the second grade and stayed with us all the way through high school. She charmed and cajoled and maneuvered us all into singing—the jocks, the nerds, the teacher's pets, and the mavericks—all of us.

And we loved her.

No single person in that little town did more to shape the boys of my generation into courteous, respectful, mannered young men than Miss South.

Even today, there are men who grew up under her caring eye who don't swear in public and rarely in private. Miss South thought swearing was the mark of a person of limited intelligence and woeful vocabulary, that civility and manners were absolute requirements of young men who respected themselves and intended to amount to something.

And you had better respect yourself.

And you better amount to something.

There are men who still open doors for women and walk on the curbside to shield them from whatever dangers the street may hold, men who, even though the ladies sometimes object, think manners are important and practice them—because she taught them so.

Most of our team sang in her school choirs or choruses and some sang in the groups she took to the state music competitions each year.

In my senior year, our boys' quartet, which included me, a fullback; Jerry South, her nephew and our center; Russ Brown, an end; and Henry Clay Gardenhire, a cheerleader, won the state championship.

In my yearbook, she wrote:
> *Here's to my winning quartet.*
> *As dear boys as I've ever met.*
> *To my handsome young bass,*
> *there is always a place*
> *in my heart.*
> *May he never forget.*

I have never had a thing written me that I treasure more.

We were extraordinarily fortunate to have people like Miss South around us and to be in a place like Frankfort as we were growing up. The adults and the teachers there cared.

The town was small then, small enough that most people knew each other, and if they didn't know you, they knew your parents or knew someone who knew your parents. You felt that if you needed help, there was an adult around somewhere who'd give it. You knew, also, if you misbehaved noticeably, someone would know and was likely to let your parents know. You did not want that to happen.

But if you excelled at something, they'd know that, too, and there would be smiles of approval and nods of the head. Which made you feel proud. Your parents, too.

The psychologists call this sort of thing positive reinforcement. The town itself was positive reinforcement.

You could skate on the sidewalks and ride your bike and not be worried about being run over. It was okay to play out after dark. We played kick-the-can in the neighborhood streets on summer nights by the light of corner lampposts. In winter, when the snow came, we made bonfires at the top of Capitol Hill and rode our sleds all the way from the Capitol down to the river.

When were older, we walked our dates home on quiet sidewalks full of moonlight and shadows.

Farmland surrounded the town and rolling Bluegrass pastures where thoroughbred yearlings played. We could swim in the river and fish Elkhorn Creek for smallmouth in one of the finest bass streams in the whole southeast.

There were sock hops every Saturday night at the YMCA (no shoes allowed on the gym floor) and dances at the Episcopal Parish House on autumn Fridays after home games.

There was never the thought that danger lurked or trouble waited.

Poverty and crime and suffering and want existed, of course, but these weren't the things I saw growing up, or not enough of them to make a conscious impression. My father saw them and he fought against them, but they didn't intrude on my days or nights.

You felt confident in the place. You could trust it. You could trust the people around you. That was reassuring. It gave us a solid base.

We needed that.

We were born in the years of the Great Depression.

That was a hard time for our parents. Money was tight. The outlook grim. But not much of that worry rubbed off on us. They tried to see to that. My father sold his books in order to buy my Christmas presents one year, my Mother later told me.

World War II began as we were finishing fourth grade.

We knew shortages and rationing and air-raid drills and somber-voiced men on the radio telling us how our boys were off in strange places fighting evil men to save us and the civilized world.

When we got to high school, the atomic age dawned. The specter of a formidable bomb that would spawn mutant monsters and wipe out whole cities haunted our dreams and sent some scurrying to build bomb shelters to shield their families from the consequences.

The Korean War exploded the summer we graduated high school.

The Cold War, with its threat of World War III, loomed menacingly over our college years.

There were only sixty-three of us. Twenty-nine stayed home. Fourteen wandered to other parts of the Commonwealth. The rest wound up in more distant climes—one all the way up to Alaska.

One girl became a high-ranking officer in the Salvation Army. Our quarterback ran one of the nation's most successful textile firms. Another was vice president of the town's biggest bank. Several became senior executives of Fortune 500 companies. There were engineers and teachers and merchants and salesmen and secretaries and stay-at-home moms, and civil servants taking care of the business of the people as managers of departments of state government.

One undertaker.

No preachers, though.

I can't account for that.

When the class got around to naming favorites, the quarterback, Jackie Moore, was voted most popular. Gordon Taylor, a guard, the bank vice president mentioned above, was chosen as the best-looking boy. His nickname was Peaches. He had a peaches and cream complexion that all the girls envied. Joan Hutcherson was the most popular girl and the best dancer. She married Gordon.

Jerry South was the most dependable. He went on to lead one of Bank of America's major divisions. Martha Watts, a pretty blonde with elfin grace, was named most talented—and biggest flirt. We all flirted with her but she didn't date any of us. She came from a strict, religious family. We didn't think we'd pass muster.

Jane McDonald was voted prettiest and Barbara Cardwell cutest, Roe Rogers the best sport, and Billy D. McDonald (no relation to Jane) the class president and boy with the best disposition.

Roe, at the very least, was complicit in the plot that closed the whole school down one frigid winter morning.

Although he contends to this day that the honor should go to Bobby Lancaster, who played end on our team and was a co-conspirator with Roe in many diabolic escapades, the fact remains that there was plenty of glory to be shared. In the grip of some inspiration never divulged, one of them slipped a block of Limburger cheese onto the school radiator down in the furnace room.

The fragrance that floated upward filled the halls and the classrooms with an aroma so gag-inducing that the principal, F. D. Wilkinson, a disciplinarian not to be trifled with, had no alternative but to suspend school for the rest of the day and send us all home.

Wilkie never fingered the culprit. It was one of his biggest disappointments. Roe later became a very high official in Kentucky state government.

You already know about Monk.

I've often thought the most successful one among us didn't graduate with us.

He was slower than the rest, but unwaveringly cheerful. He had a fine bass voice and sometimes sang solos in our school recitals. He willingly did anything he could to be helpful, tried so hard that even the hard-asses among us gave him grudging respect.

Of all the ones I knew, he made the most of what he had.

If you're wondering why I mention all these people whose names may mean nothing to you, it is because they deserve to be remembered.

Humor me.

The F Club, the lettermen's club

Gordon Taylor is third from the left in the first row. I'm next to
him on the right. Jackie Moore is next me and Monk Hudson is next
to Jackie. Jerry South is on the end of that row. Russ Brown is in
the row behind Jerry (in the letter jacket). Roe Rogers is first on
the left in the third row and Bobby Lancaster is the fourth from
the left in the fourth row.

The others are part of this story, too, just not identified by name
in the text.

I've left little Frankfort-nestled-among-the-hills now and
ventured out into the big, blue-eyed world.
I've made it from boy to man now.
A country boy.
Wandering
Wondering.

Wonderer

Mostly we followed the roads that ran beside the rivers.

From San Francisco Bay, we headed north across the delta and up along the broad Sacramento, flowing milky green and ice-cold from snow melt off the Siskiyou mountains.

At the capital we left the wide river and turned east, easing up through the Gold Country and onto the western slope of the Sierra.

The South Fork of the Yuba and the main branch of the American bracketed us for a while, the Yuba on our left, the American on our right. We caught occasional glances of white water tumbling over boulders and coasting into riffles—water that gave up fortunes in gold in the old days and gives up some even now to a tamer breed of prospector panning gravel on holidays and weekends.

We crested the Sierra at Donner Summit and picked up the Truckee just north of Lake Tahoe.

The stretch of the river there is primarily pocket water where long casts are useless. Trout are smart. Rather than fight the current, they lie protected from the rush of the water in eddies behind half sunken boulders and submerged logs, waiting. Only strong waders can reach these holds. Only bold waders try.

The Truckee runs through the center of the town that bears its name. East of the city limit there is a trophy section where really big rainbow wait. It's catch and release. Flies only. Single hook. Barbless.

Chris kept his gaze out the window, trying to catch glimpses of it through the pines as we rode by.

The river cuts the freeway in five places in the ten miles between Truckee and the Nevada line. Long stretches can be seen and wondered about and, in turn, give rise to speculation about other waters.

"What do you think we'll find?"

I looked over.

His gaze was still toward the river.

"At the Big Hole? Fishing so good that even you might be able to hang one," I said, laughing.

This was the first long trip we'd taken together since his fifteenth birthday four years ago. At that time, he had just gotten his driver's permit and we set off to test it and to see the country, sharing the drive on a long looping circuit from San Francisco Bay, where we lived, to the Bluegrass of Kentucky, where I grew up, and back again. We swung out through the moonscape of the high deserts and back through the grasses of the Great Plains and the peaks of the Rockies.

This trip was something of a gamble for us both—father and son alone on a three-week trek with nothing but the landscape, the radio, and each other's company to entertain us.

There had been overnight fishing trips and family vacations before but nothing which kept us together over so extended a time and on such an individual basis. Before, he had been a child and my role was clearly parental—guiding, teaching, in authority. Now we were moving into a different relationship—not yet man to man, but no longer man to boy.

"Usual bet?" Chris said. "Five bucks across. First. Biggest. Most."

"You're going to risk fifteen dollars and bragging rights when you know it's no contest? I'll hang the first, land the biggest, and no question about who'll catch the most."

A snort, a laugh.

"Let you off easy," he said. "Give me five now and save yourself the embarrassment."

We were running down the eastern flank of the Sierra with Nevada just ahead.

We had discovered on that first long trip that we were companionable. We were easy in each other's company.

Now, some four years later with his graduation from an eastern university just two weeks behind us, we were treating ourselves to another long trip and were off to fish the storied waters of the Big Hole River of Montana.

We stayed with the Truckee out onto the Nevada plain and kept east as the river turned north. This is high desert country, sage-brushed, gullied, and dry. Names of waterless streambeds are announced with bold road signs. Towns along the straight reach of the interstate have initials cut large onto the most prominent hillside. Civic pride in moonscape land.

At Elko we turned left and north again, heading for Ketchum across the Great Gorge of the Snake River. The river has cut a massive canyon there just outside Twin Falls. A long bridge spans it and far below the Snake looks as small as a shoestring laid on the bottom of the canyon. Evel Knievel tried to jump it on his motorcycle once. After they swept him up from the floor of the gorge, it took him almost sixteen months to mend his shattered bones.

At Ketchum I wanted to see where Hemingway had lived his last years and where he lay.

And I wanted to fish his Big Wood River.

Hemingway died while we were in Ravenswood.

He shot himself.

A Sunday morning, in his home in Ketchum, not quite eight o'clock.

He was in his pajamas and robe. He leaned his forehead against his favorite double-barrel shotgun, a Boss 12-guage, and blew the top of his head off.

His wife was asleep.

The fact of the suicide greatly saddened me. I have no brief for or against suicide. If pain or despair so afflict a person that he chooses to end it and has the will to do so, the choice should be his, free of the moralizing of those not bearing the burden. The consequences of the act, though, fall to all of us.

It seemed wrong that Hemingway had killed himself. Nature should have gotten him.

Or chance.

But not his own deliberate action, not with his own gun, in his own hand, as the day came awake on a peaceful Sunday morning.

He had earned a better passing.

I liked what I thought I knew of the man. I liked that he was a fisherman and a hunter and did these things well and understood what they were about. I liked that he had been a newspaperman and wrote journalism throughout his career. I liked that he seemed to have clear values and stood by them. And I liked the stories he told and the way he told them.

I had been a latecomer to Hemingway. Thomas Wolfe and Stephen Vincent Benét and a grab bag of other storytellers and wordsmiths spoke more to my needs and my interests earlier on.

I had, of course, read the requisite Hemingway in school, but I preferred others. Then, for some reason, in Ravenswood, I began to reread Hemingway. *Big Two-Hearted River; A Clean, Well-Lighted Place; The Old Man and the Sea,* especially *Big Two-Hearted River.* I liked the short stories better than the novels, but I admired the man who wrote them all.

We had been in Ravenswood, on the Great Bend of the Ohio River, in West Virginia, for about two years when Hemingway died. This was the first home in our young marriage outside Kentucky. For Patsy, it was her first time away. As a child, with my family, I had lived in California and Alabama and Florida. This was during the years of World War II, and my father, who was in his thirties and just past war age, edited newspapers in these places. There was a shortage of qualified journalists at that time and this allowed him to indulge his wanderer's curiosity, looking for better opportunities and bigger challenges.

Even so, it was not a long diaspora, three years, perhaps a little more.

Home drew us.

My father was born and grew up in Frankfort, as did I and my younger sister, Ann, and my brother, Donnie. Mary Lou, the youngest, was born in California; the happiest of our stops and the place where we all would have been raised if my mother had her way, but his urge to try new ground was too strong, so we moved on.

Even though we roamed, Frankfort had a powerful pull on all of us. My father was constantly tempted by greener pastures, but I think he would never have left it for good.

This pull is hard to explain. It is more than a matter of the familiar or the comfortable. It is the feeling of belonging.

At the time I was growing up there, its population was under fifteen thousand. Though it is the capital of the Grand and Glorious Commonwealth of Kentucky, it is not a large town even now. But it has character and power. If roads are to be built, jobs awarded, contracts let, taxes levied or relieved, Frankfort is where it happens. If the whole machinery that runs the counties and the state is to be fueled, maintained, and driven, Frankfort is at the controls.

Secure in this knowledge, the town snuggles in a peaceful river valley in the heart of the Bluegrass. It was a place of wide, tree-lined streets and quiet neighborhoods, elegant old mansions and comfortable houses with broad lawns and swings on front porches.

The Capitol itself is a copy of the U.S. Capitol in Washington. But its setting is more majestic. It looks out over the city from a gentle hill above the residential section south of the river.

The other Capitol, the Old Capitol, sits in that leafy square in the center of town. At night, bathed in soft lights, it seems the sort of place where magic could be made.

Perhaps it was this mix of the power and excitement of politics overlaid with the sheer physical charm of the town that kept drawing my father back.

But I think it was more than that.

I think it was the idea of home.

The Scots-Irish of the southeastern states seem to feel this most, some marker in the blood that draws them home.

My people are of this blood—Irish and Welsh on my father's side, English and Scots on my mother's.

My father's people, the Rhodys and the Owens, were townspeople

My mother's people, the Clarks and the Edwards, were farmers. She was one of ten—six boys and four girls. She was the next to youngest.

There are tons of Clarks and many Taylors—aunts, uncles, cousins. Not so many Rhodys. My dad was one of two—himself and a younger brother.

Even so, I sometimes think I could return and run for state legislature and get elected on family vote alone.

About all that my mother and her sisters knew about the man named Taylor Edwards, their mother's father, their grandfather, was that he "came from somewhere up in the mountains," and he spoke with a strong Scottish burr.

He appeared mysteriously out of the morning fog one spring day, riding a raft of logs downriver, so the story goes.

Frankfort had busy sawmills in those days and that's the way the men of the Cumberland forests got their timber to market. They roped the freshly cut logs into big rafts and rode them on spring floods down the Kentucky River to the sawmills in the Bluegrass.

It took strength and skill to steer the raft of logs through the stick-ups and the rapids of the rushing river. And courage. A hand or a leg could be lost in the blink of an eye. You could be thrown off in the shifts of the rapids and drown trying to swim out.

Taylor Edwards was a riverman.

He met Sally Baxter at a dance the night after the raft he was guiding made the Frankfort landing. The town staged the dances regularly when the loggers came down. She caught his eye with the flash of her smile and the swish of her skirt.

"I'm gonna marry that gal," he told his buddy.

He wooed her with the promise that her feet would never touch cold floors.

My mother and her sisters adored him.

Taylor Edwards was full of fun and had that special gentleness that, as if in recompense for their size and strength, a few big men have. He loved children and indulged them. On Sundays, after they'd married and he'd left the river and become a farmer and they'd had children of their own and all the family gathered for Sunday dinner at the Edwards place, he was the first into the games.

"Taylor, you're the biggest child in the bunch," his wife would scold, eyes flashing and disapproving as he wrestled with the boys in the grass.

"Now stop all that, all of you, and get ready for supper." Wiping her hands on her apron, she would move back off the porch to watch as, still laughing and jostling, Taylor Edwards and the boys headed for the pump to wash up outside.

Great Grandmother Sally Edwards was not adored. The children thought her a flinty woman with a stern disposition.

But he loved her and he kept his promise. On cold mornings, he would rise before daylight, get a fire started in the old woodstove, heat a small rug over it, and place it, warmed and waiting, by her side of the bed. While he was alive, her feet never touched cold floors.

My mother's other grandmother, her Clark grandmother, was dearly loved and lived with my mother's family when my mother was a little girl…and died with them at home … in her son's wife's arms.

My mom remembered it.

That day was cold—ground-creaking cold. Steam rose from the porch posts and the tin roof of the farmhouse as the sun warmed them.

The breakfast dishes were left undone. My mother and her sisters were ringed around the edges of the large featherbed in their grandmother's room. A few were sniffling quietly. They all were frightened and uncertain. They were farm children and they had seen death before, but never the death of a person, never the death of a loved one. They were trying their hardest not to cry out loud.

The room was full of light from the morning sun. Dry corn stalks were rustling in the wind and shadows cast by the big locust tree outside played on the wall.

My mother's mother was crying softly. She was up in the bed, sitting with her back against the wall, holding her husband's mother in her arms. One of the boys had been sent to the barn to get him. When he came into the room, heavy coat still on, boots wet with melting frost, he moved directly to the bed. The children's attention locked on him. The room went quiet. He reached out to touch his mother's cheek, stroked her hair, looked questioningly at his wife. He leaned down to kiss them both. He said not a word. Then turned and left.

The family grieves awhile, each with his or her own memories and sorrows. Then they start the practical things that have to be done. Lay out the body. Wait for word to circulate among the neighbors and friends and for them to arrive.

By then it is coming on to night...a night colder than the day, but so clear the stars seem as bright as little moons. The wagons and buggies begin to arrive. Women rush from them through the cold to the warmth of the house. They hug and cry and begin to unload the food they've brought—more food than an army can consume. The tables will groan under the best that each of the comforting families can prepare until well after the funeral.

The men, not knowing what to do or how to comfort, talk quietly together or go outside to smoke on the porch in the sobering cold.

The day for the burying is one of those achingly clear ones, with a stillness that only a numbing cold can command and a sky so blue it seems almost white. By mid-morning, the sun has softened the ground enough that they can get shovels into it. They dig the grave in the thawing earth and lower her gently down. A verse is read, a hymn started. The women's voices are strong and clear, the men's tentative and rumbly. A lonely breeze, the first of the day, catches the melody and floats it out from the little country cemetery over the surrounding fields.

After the service ends, my grandmother and grandfather stand by the graveside taking final condolences. The men shake hands. The women embrace. My grandfather Clark, in his only suit, nods, mumbles thank yous. He is tightly held in. Grown men don't show emotion.

When all have left, he and my grandmother turn and walk through the long shadows back to their buggy. My grandmother has long black hair caught up in a bun at the back of her neck. Her strong body and easy grace give comfort just in her bearing. She hints of Cherokee blood.

My grandfather beside her, tall but no taller than she, walks rapidly as if to out-walk the pain. My mother trails them, crying.

Who was she, this woman they lay in the cold, cold ground that winter day? What did she want? What did she get?

No answers.

The mysterious young boy whose name was Roddy, or O'Roddy, maybe Rhody—immigration officials wrote down what they thought they heard through the brogue—was about sixteen when he came.

Alone.

We don't know what tragedy or hopes sent him out.

He would have been a child during the great potato famine in Ireland, would have seen the starvation, probably experienced the pain, the shame, the despair of it.

Where in Ireland was his home? Why did he come alone? Did all the family die and he, the only survivor, escape to America? Or was he the youngest, and if only one passage could be afforded, was he the chosen one?

They say he never heard from or communicated with any family in Ireland.

Was there some sinister reason for his leaving, something that made him an outcast?

The first record turns up in the marriage book of St. Joseph's Roman Catholic Church in Bowling Green, Kentucky, on the occasion of the marriage of Patrick Roddy, or O'Roddy (it is noted both ways) to Elizabeth Majors on April 13, 1860.

This is the one who brought our set of Rhody genes to America.

In the 1860s, Bowling Green was a small market town in western Kentucky, a considerable way from any port of entry and seemingly a place of far less attraction for a young Irishman than, say, New York or Baltimore or Philadelphia. Why did he wind up in Bowling Green?

And why did he make his way up to the Bluegrass and Frankfort?

He would have been four years in this country when the Civil War broke out. Kentucky was a deeply divided state, perhaps the most divided in that war, the one state that truly did pit brother against brother and father against son.

The crucial battle for the control of Kentucky was fought about thirty miles south of Frankfort, at Perryville. The Confederates came up through west Kentucky, crossing the border from Tennessee and moving up past Bowling Green into the central part of the state. Did they pull him along?

Whatever his role in that war and however he came to Frankfort, Patrick O'Roddy, now Rhody, and Elizabeth Majors have nine children—three girls and six boys—one of whom, Bernard, was my grandfather.

Bernard and his wife Annie Owens, the young Welsh girl we know so little about, have two children, two boys. The eldest, James Bernard, is my father.

James Bernard, "Bummy" to his friends, was a handsome young man with wavy black hair, strikingly deep blue eyes, and a tenor voice so pure that he was regularly asked to sing with the big bands when they came touring through the Bluegrass.

People liked to be around him.

He wound up a newspaperman, one of the last of the crusading breed.

He died on his feet arguing for the rights of blacks to use a new municipal swimming pool that was being built in our town at a time and in a state where desegregation had not yet had its moment.

A heart attack. He was just recovering from an earlier one. His doctor cautioned him not to go.

"If it kills me, I have to be there," he said to my mother. He was forty-six.

This happened at a town meeting in the local high school auditorium. Most of the town was there.

I was in my junior year at the University of Kentucky, living at home then, commuting up to Lexington each day, and working part-time at the local radio station. It was fairly late in the evening, ten o'clock or so.

I don't remember who told us.

I know it wasn't a phone call. Someone, surely a family friend who knew us well, must have come to the door and told us. But I don't remember who it was or what was said. The whole night is a blur to me.

I do remember making the long walk with my brother through the quiet streets from the funeral home where they had taken his body.

It was an April night, clear and cool, but with enough warmth in the air to know spring was close. The maples were just coming into full leaf. Donnie was about eleven then. Although he tried his best not to, he cried most of the way back. I can hear him even now and feel my arm around his shoulders. The streets were dark except for the corners where the streets lights stood. He tried to cry only where it was dark, so that no one would see him. The dark helped cradle his hurt.

I didn't cry then.

Later that night, after the others were in bed, I walked down to the foot of our street. There was a broad lawn of grass and trees off to the side of the Capitol building that was bordered by an old stone wall. It was dark and secluded there. No one around. I sat on the grass with my back against that wall and did my crying there.

I didn't cry again.

My father's death changed everything for us.

To me it brought responsibilities I hadn't had before. Newspapermen in those days had prestige, but not much money. I decided rather than continue to law school at UK, to which I had been accepted, I should get through school and get a full-time job as rapidly as possible to help with the needs of the family.

My father was a dreamer and a crusader. He was of that breed to whom journalism is a calling, as the ministry is a calling.

He believed that wrongs must be righted and truths be told. He believed the weak must be protected and the powerful held in check. He used his newspaper to try to do that. His tombstone carries a line written in a note to my mother after his death by one of the people he had helped. It reads, "He spoke for those who cannot speak."

Some of my earliest memories are of being with him at the *Journal*—the *Frankfort State Journal*, the paper on which he was first a reporter, then columnist, and later and finally, its managing editor.

From the time my mother would let him (I know I was still not old enough for school) he would take me with him on Saturday nights. The newsroom at night was a magical place, full of noise and excitement. Typewriters chattered and phones rang and reporters rushed in and out. We would watch as the teletypes spewed out news from all over the world and walk through the backshop where linotype machines were turning the words the reporters wrote into silver slugs of type that would be locked into page forms which would become the morning newspaper. And later we would make paper balls of crumpled newsprint bound by rubber bands and shoot baskets at the waste cans in the newsroom.

And then, when Page One was locked up, we would walk home through the silent streets with the whole city asleep, feeling that there were only the two of us and it belonged to us alone. That gave me so proud a feeling that I sometimes couldn't get to sleep for what seemed like hours, even after Mom, who was always waiting up, had quieted me down and put me to bed.

I made my way through the chairs at the *Journal* working for, and with, my father, after school and part-time, first as a reporter, then as a sports writer, and lastly, in the year or so just before his death, shepherding the Sunday morning paper on to the press.

I was doing that, and pulling night shifts at the local radio station to help pay my way through school, when he died.

So I didn't go lawyering.

Instead, I was in Ravenswood, West (by God) Virginia, a quiet little town of about three thousand where I worked for a large multinational aluminum company that had built the world's largest aluminum complex at the Great Bend of the Ohio River.

This was the second-best job I ever had.

The best was for the Kentucky Department of Fish and Wildlife Resources. I wrote for the monthly outdoors magazine and created a weekly radio and television show called "Kentucky Afield." I hunted in the best spots in the state and fished the best waters and got to meet and know of some of the finest people in the Commonwealth.

It was a grand time, but Patsy grew tired of eating rabbit and bass, and I was restless for bigger challenges.

We had married about a year after my father's death. I was just finishing at the University of Kentucky and she was in her sophomore year at Webster College, a girls' school in St. Louis.

Though we had both grown up in Frankfort, she was one of the Catholic girls. She went to the local parochial school rather than the grade schools and high schools the children of our predominantly Protestant town attended. I didn't meet her until I was in college.

Then, one sunny Sunday morning, standing on Pete's Corner after church, the most strikingly pretty girl I had ever seen came walking by. I don't remember the color of her dress or the names of the girls who were with her.

All I remember is her face, and the wide-brimmed white straw hat that framed it.

I learned her name from a friend and called her that afternoon—which led, among many other things, to three delightful daughters and the son in my company on this trip to the Big Hole.

Patsy was playing bridge at a neighbor's house and I was home the night the news about Hemingway came.

The report didn't register at first.

Only half listening to the television as I did something or other in the kitchen, the words began to gradually sink in and I walked slowly around the countertop that edged the den to stand in front of the television screen.

The girls were asleep. The house was dark except for the kitchen light and a lone lamp lit in the den.

The reporter moved from the news of Hemingway's death into a hastily assembled tribute on his life—old film clips, the reminiscences of friends and admirers, readings from his works.

And I was saddened.

I had a very good start on a promising career, enjoyed what I was doing, did it well, and was well paid for it. But I began to wonder if I had let something more important slip away.

I didn't discuss this with anyone. Career kept distracting me. New challenges came, and with them came new opportunities, more responsibility ... and more money.

We were promoted to New York, and then to corporate headquarters in California, and I moved fairly rapidly up the ladder. There was too much in sight to be distracted by wondering what might have been.

I didn't think about this in any serious way until Carlos Baker's biography of Hemingway came out.

And then I wanted to visit Hemingway's grave at Ketchum and decided to route us through there on our trip to the Big Hole.

Hemingway and his wife Mary are buried in the small cemetery on the north edge of Ketchum. The cemetery is so small that I missed finding it on my first attempt.

An afternoon thunderstorm blew up just as we arrived. The air became ozone charged. Lightening stabbed at the mountaintops across the valley and rain, a hard driving rain that obliterated all vision, pounded down.

We stayed in the car and waited for the storm to pass and the serene blue sky of the summer Rockies to appear again.

The gate leading to the Ketchum cemetery was topped by a black wrought-iron arch supported by two columns of stone. Through it, and out onto the wet grass, we began to search for his grave.

There were no markers, no special notice. The grave was not announced. It was well toward the rear, almost in the center, modestly marked. There was no headstone, just a gray granite slab laid flat on the ground with the dates of his coming and going inscribed.

The Hemingway Memorial at Sun Valley was equally unpretentious—just a small bronze bust on a pedestal beside a narrow stream on a hillside above the valley of the Big Wood. He is looking upstream, scanning the water as a fisherman would.

After we left Ketchum, Chris and I fished the Big Wood through aspen groves and pine stands. We didn't hang a thing, but it was good just to feel the water around our legs and make the casts.

Then we pushed on up over Galena Summit and down into the valley of the Salmon River.

Rain sat in and stayed with us as we moved north to Chief Joseph Pass. We turned east there, crossed the Continental Divide, and began the long glide into the vast bowl at the foot of the Bitterroots that the mountain men called The Big Hole.

The river that waters this plain takes its name from the place. It is majestic country—mountain ringed, brilliantly green, awesomely quiet. It is secluded and uncrowded and some of the best fishing I'd ever had.

We headquartered outside the little town of Wise River in a snug cabin with a riffle at our door close enough to walk down to and make casts before breakfast. We worked the stream in both directions, wading sometimes, but most often casting from a drift boat, always over beautiful water.

We played rainbows and brookies and cutthroats and browns. Except for an occasional afternoon thunderstorm, the days were warm and clear and the nights cold and crisp. There was a full moon so big it filled half the sky and a rainstorm more intense than any I had ever witnessed.

And strong, wild fish that hit hard and fought heroically.

We fished for five days, landed twenty-one on one day alone.

We didn't keep a fish. Their fight and their beauty earned them their return to the stream.

When the time came to leave, Chris pocketed his winnings and the bragging rights and we ran south with the Big Hole for a way, then cut west and headed back to the valley of the Snake.

We bypassed Ketchum.

I had seen what I wanted to see there.

And I had an answer to a question I hadn't known I'd asked.

II

MARKERS

This is as far as I got.

I've shifted into neutral now.

Motor idling.

Considering.

It isn't because I'm not famous or that this story is not unique.

It's that as I reach back remembering, I'm not sure I want to.

Once the remembering starts—serious remembering—the spigot opens. Memories push their way in unbidden, some so pleasurable I don't want to leave them. Some so troubling I'd like them erased.

I'm idling, considering.

Even so, there are some things that should be recorded now so that they are not forgotten.

Into That Good Night

The First Baptist Church of Frankfort is at the foot of the bridge that joins the two halves of the town.

The church has been there since 1876.

We grew up in it. The place is as familiar to us any house we ever lived in.

Donnie and Ann and Mary Lou and their families, are already there when we arrive.

We've come in from California—me and Patsy and our children. Not children anymore. Kath has her doctorate in psychology and has started Orion Academy, the country's first high school for children with Asperger's Syndrome, Meg is making it run smoothly as the administrative manager, Kim has traded in her post as public defender in the Oakland DA's office to concentrate on raising Riley and the twins, and Chris is establishing his own law practice in Denver.

All the Clarks in driving distance are there.

And the ladies of her Sunday School class, and most of the rest of the congregation, and other friends from around town and the county.

All have come to say their farewells to Matt ... to Mary Mathew ... to Mom.

It is a fine spring morning and sunlight spills through stained glass windows. The church is full of flowers. The casket is in the front of the church, centered below the pulpit.

Several have been asked to speak.
I am the last.

"This is intended to be a celebration, not a sad time. A time for thinking good thoughts and remembering good times.

And no life gave us more of those than Mom's.

But this is an emotional family. There has been some crying. There will be crying still. And that's okay. If the Lord hadn't meant for us to cry when there was reason to cry, he wouldn't have given us tears.

I may even cry before this is over. If I do, I know you'll bear with me.

She lived a good life.

At times it was hard.

And at times, even though there were a lot of us around, it must have been awfully lonely. She was so young when Dad died. But she had a good life because she refused to have it any other way.

She always found the best in things.

She always found the best in people.

And loved them for it.

If you were lucky enough to know her, you couldn't help but love her.

She dealt with what came to her.

And made the best of it. Without complaint.

She used to say me, "The Lord has been good to this Rhody family, Ronnie. He's been good to us."

We know that's true… because he gave us her.

And there was always her laughter.

She could always make us laugh.

And the stories…lord, the stories. There must be a laughter gene somewhere in the Clark DNA. Anytime they got together, anywhere they got together, in any number—two or three or the whole Clark clan—it was stories and laughter.

And even though there may be some crying still, it will be the same today—laughter and stories and good times remembered.

I've never been around a group who enjoyed each other more than Mom's Clarks. And I've never been around anyone who loved her family more, or who loved children more, or who loved fun more, than Mom.

She had many very special gifts.

Those of you who have seen the pictures, know that she was a strikingly beautiful young woman... and that beauty stayed with her.

She was brave and determined and very strong, but very gentle.

The real thing, though, was her gift for love.

If you were lucky enough that she knew you, she loved you. And if you were lucky enough to know her, you loved her.

She kept her great spirit right up to the end.

During the last few weeks she was very ill at times and of course she didn't want to worry anyone.

One day when she was being actively ill and Mary Lou was with her, one of Mary Lou's daughters called. The daughter wanted to know why Nanny was throwing up. "Oh, just tell her I'm pregnant," Mom said.

Closer to the end, Kathy, my eldest, was with her. The good people at Hospice, and they are good, wonderful people, felt that perhaps Mom was hanging on because of her concern about us and that we should let her know it would be all right to let go.

But that wasn't it.

She was hanging on because she wanted to get well and keep living.

She told my daughter Kathy, "When the time comes, I'm ready. But if the good Lord wants me, he's going to have to come get me."

Finally He did.

On a beautiful clear, cold night in May with a half moon riding in a cloudless sky....in her own home...in her own bed...with many of her family around her...peacefully...the way she wanted it.

For those of us who are her children—Ann and Mary Lou and Donnie and me—I want to say that we are fortunate beyond belief to have had her. And she has given us riches beyond measure by the bounty of her love.

There is a song she liked. An old English ballad with a lovely tune. It begins, "There is a lady, sweet and kind. Was never face so pleased my mind. I did but see her passing by. Yet will I love her 'til I die."

We do.

We will."

Ann, Mom, and Mary Lou

So Mom died.

That we were adults made no difference.
We were children again and the hurt was deep. It lingers.
Do not believe it when you are told time heals all wounds.
All time does is dull the pain.
But life went on.
As it should.
As it does.

Then,

and it wasn't proper, for she was the youngest and the fairest and the delight of us all,

Mary Lou died.

Sing No Sad Songs

A Thursday in July.

Sultry, but enough breeze to temper the humidity.

Skies clear, roses blooming on a trellis by the door.

Lovely day.

We're in Shelbyville.

Nice town. Pleasant town. About twenty miles from Frankfort on the road to Louisville. Our archrival when I was in school.

Mary Lou has lived here since her marriage.

She had her children here, made her home here where her husband had his factory.

Her daughters have asked me to be part of the service, to speak of her, not understanding how impossible it will be to account for Mary Lou with mere words.

"There are three things I know I must not do in these next few minutes:

I must not be sad. I must not be maudlin. And I must not talk very long.

Mary Lou would not be happy with that.

She is the only one of us who wasn't born in Kentucky.

She was born in California, in a little mining and lumbering town called Yreka up in the Siskiyou Mountains near the Oregon border. I remember Donnie and Ann and me crowding into the room in that little hospital to see her for the first time.

She didn't look very pretty to us then…but she grew into one of the loveliest women I've ever seen.

And I remember that long train ride back across the country when she was only a month or so old, coming home to Kentucky…and all the people beaming at her.

She had that effect on people…even then.

I don't think there has ever been anyone who generated so much happiness and energy as Mary Lou. She was effervescent…incandescent. She sparkled. All the time. Everywhere. She infected you. You couldn't be around her and hold on to a bad mood. She had fun. She spread it.

I know she had hard times. But she handled whatever came her way without complaint and she didn't offload her troubles or her worries on others. She had a good heart, a brave heart.

It is a high compliment for any of us to be considered good at something. She was good at all the things that count— mother, wife, sister, daughter, friend—good at them all.

The way she conducted herself in dying is something that I admire more than I can find words for.

She didn't feel sorry for herself. She didn't want others to feel sorry for her either. She kept her spirit all the way, savoring every minute she was given and taking every ounce of joy she could squeeze out of the time she got to spend with her family and friends.

In the dying, she lived.

I saw her cry only once.

Several weeks before she passed, while she was still able to get out a bit, she and Donnie and I took a long drive out Shady Lane. It was one of those picture-perfect Bluegrass summer afternoons: fluffy white clouds floating in a bright blue sky and throwing moving shadows on the fields…a light breeze ruffling the tops of the trees. We talked and told family stories and laughed.

At one point, though, she turned to me and said, "Don't you let them say I lost my fight. Don't you let them say that!" She began to cry then. "I'm not losing a fight. I'm finishing my journey."

Well, honey, you finished the journey...with so much courage and class that we all are in awe.

One other story, then I'll stop.

I'm a bit reluctant to tell it because I may not get through it. And you may take it too sentimentally.

I don't mean it that way.

I mean it as a closing picture of her wonderful spirit and I want you to consider it as a moment of triumph, not a moment of loss.

The last time I saw her alive was several weeks ago. It was morning, a lovely June morning, clear and cool and full of bird song. I had been here on a short visit to see her and stopped by on my way back to the airport. She was in her bed in her room upstairs at her home in Shelbyville. We all knew time was running out.

I sat and we talked for a while...and laughed...and enjoyed each other's company.

When it came time for me to go, I got up, leaned over and kissed her on the cheek, and walked to the door. When I reached it, I opened it and turned around briefly to look back.

She was sitting up against the pillows, watching me. She smiled that wonderful smile of hers. And blew me a kiss.

That's an image I'll hold.

Not in sadness, but in love.

So, honey, we'll sing no sad songs...and weep no longer than we must.

We'll just be thankful for the time we had."

Then Ann.

Too soon. It's all too soon.

We don't pay enough attention.
We let time slip away while we're focused on chimeras and delusions.
We listen but don't hear.
We look but don't see.

Pay attention.

Good Night Sweetheart

The church is full to overflowing, It sits on a corner in a tranquil Frankfort neighborhood of well keep houses and quite streets. Outside, the air is misty and there is a chill in it, but inside it's warm and peaceful. The only sounds are those of people settling in their seats and the organ playing softly.

Her two grandsons will speak, and her son-in-law, and me.

The pastor first. He knows her. They are friends.

Then we'll all file out and follow the hearse across the river on this autumn morning and up the hill to the cemetery. There will be words spoken there, and tears and hugs, and that part of it will be over.

I don't want to have to do this again.

I don't want, ever again, to stand beside a casket and try to find the words, to find the words and speak them, at the passing of a loved one or a friend. We will all die. I know this. It is the natural order of things and to be accepted and honored.

I know all this. Still....

"There were four of us.

Ann, Mary Lou, Donnie, and me.

We were very close...in a comfortingly protective sort of way.

That stemmed, I think, from the "travels."

When we were young—I was about eleven, Ann about seven, Donnie about four, Mary Lou not born yet, but she came along shortly and made the rest of the trip with us—we began a time of wandering.

Out across the country to Yreka, a small town in Northern California,

—then back across the country to Mobile in Alabama,

—and to Tallahassee in Florida for short while,

—and down to Sarasota,

—and back up to Dothan in Alabama.

Our Dad was a newspaper editor and he went newspapering in all those places.

During that time, we seemed to be moving almost constantly—into towns where we knew no one and no one knew us—never staying long enough anywhere to get any real sense of belonging.

That experience, coming as it did when we were so young, caused us to bond even closer than we might have under more ordinary circumstances.

Being dropped down into unfamiliar places among strangers caused us to realize that the people we could count on were *us* … to know that the place where we were certain to be welcome and safe was in that little circle of *us*.

We came back to Frankfort after a while and finished our growing up here. Later, when I started chasing opportunities in new towns out among other strangers, I always felt very secure. The experience of those years is the reason, because when we became adults and began to go our own ways, I knew that no matter what happened, my own little circle of *us* was there for me, would comfort and protect and sustain, would be sanctuary…regardless.

That feeling has never gone away. And it has been a great strength for me.

I had an email the other day from Kitty Simcox—Kitty Hanley when we were growing up here. Some of you may remember her. She lives in Golden, Colorado, and had heard of what was happening with Ann.

Kitty wrote, "I sympathize with you having Ann die. It is hard losing one of the few people who love you unconditionally. She did. She was a lovely person. I wish I had a sister like her. I had John Booe and I miss him all the time."

And from Jerry South. Some of you will remember him, too. Jerry and I have been friends since second grade. He's in California now.

Jerry said, "I have one of those indelible childhood memories of Ann and your Mom. Your family was living in an apartment (can't remember the location). It was after school. We were at Second Street. I knocked on the door and your Mom answered with a beautiful blue-eyed baby in her arms. She introduced us by saying, 'This is Ann, Ronnie's little sister.' It was the eyes that still flash in my memory. Ann of the blue eyes."

A beautiful blue-eyed baby girl who grew into a strikingly beautiful blue-eyed woman ... who put no conditions on her love.

I listened to hymns as I tried to put these words together... hymns we grew up with ... Mom's good old Baptist hymns—Amazing Grace, Abide With Me ... others.

Patsy had just called. She was here in Frankfort. She'd been with Reni, Ann's daughter, helping take care of Ann almost 24/7 since we'd gotten word. I was back in Pinehurst for a short time attending to a few things that had to be attended to.

It was a little after nine. A grey, dreary, drizzly morning. I cried a bit ... and smiled as I remembered...

When she was a little girl there was a song our Dad used to sing to her, an old Irish song. He had a wonderful voice, and he would sing it to her sometimes at bedtime. It was about little Annie Rooney—a pretty young girl that all the boys admired. The last line of the chorus was "Little Annie Rooney is my sweetheart." Only when he sang it to Ann, he sang "little Annie Rhody is my sweetheart."

And he'd kiss her and tell her "good night, sweetheart."

She loved it.

She'd go to sleep happy.

Each of us knew Ann in a different way. Donnie and Mary Lou and I as a sister. Dutch as a wife. Reni as a mother. Her grandchildren and great grandchildren as Gaga. You knew her as a friend.

Oh, she could frost you.

Or warm you.

Or make you glad just to be around her.

A very complex person, she.

A daughter. A sister. A wife. A mother.

A woman of skill and achievement in her time in business and in state government.

A grandmother. A great-grandmother.

A friend.

So many roles to play.

So many needs to fill.

So many expectations to rise to ... and still sustain that spark that made her her own unique self.

So many roles played so well.

I have no idea what picture you have in your mind of what happens next. Ann and I talked about this. What she saw was

Mom and Dad and Mary Lou standing there waiting … with arms open and big smiles on their faces.

Home again.

Safe.

Good night, sweetheart."

The dam at the Forks of Elkhorn

Take the fork to the south creek, some of the finest smallmouth bass fishing in the whole Southeast.

A Blue Teapot

The Frankfort Women's Club is on the corner of Wapping and Washington. When I was a boy it was the town's library where on rainy afternoons I could escape to Mt. Olympus or trail behind Hawkeye in the northern forests.

The river is just down the street, the courthouse tower in sight.

This is where we've gathered, here in the old section of town where graceful mansions rise and the famous lived.

His own house is just a few blocks further down, right at the foot of Wapping, right on the river, a beautiful view of the mighty Kentucky flowing peacefully just beyond.

Sit on his overlook, watch the water, think grand thoughts. Golden.

He's not there.
So we've come here.
Not to say goodbye.
To tell stories and relive happy times.
Nothing formal or pretentious.
Friends. Family. Relaxed.
Just his style.

"We were boys together, Charles M. Hudson, Jr., and I.

Charles M—distinguished professor of anthropology, renowned authority on native American history, author of sixteen erudite book and two historical novels.

One of the best of the best.

And a gentle man.

To most of the people who knew him as an adult he was Charlie. To those of us who were boys together, he was Monk.

He dropped into our midst in our junior year in high school, a boy from a little town up on the Kentucky River that none of us had heard of.

He was different.

He read philosophy and listened to classical music. He liked poetry and literature. He was smarter than most of us...and very shy ...and tough as hell on a football field.

We became fast friends.

Though our careers took us to different parts of the country, we stayed fast friends...through all these years. And I count myself extraordinarily lucky to have had the pleasure of his company.

Odd the things you remember from when you were boys.

A football game.

I don't remember the name of the team we were playing or the score of the game, but I remember what Monk did. Monk played guard. Gordon Taylor, who is here, was at the other guard; Roe Rogers, also here, was at tackle. Bobby Lancaster, there beside Roe, was at an end. I was at linebacker.

We had the opposing team pushed back almost to its goal line when one of their backs popped through a hole, ran right over Monk, blew past me, blew past the safety and was past midfield before we knew what had happened. It was a sure touchdown. The runner was so far down the field that nobody could catch him. None of us even considered trying.

Except Monk.

Monk picked himself up and went flying past us all. He caught that boy just short of the goal line. We couldn't believe it.

Caught that boy.

Saved the game.

Impossible.

Monk didn't believe in impossible.

And a conversation.

We were sitting one night on the wall across from Pete's Corner, talking, which we often did. Somehow the conversation worked its way around to immortality and the Tibetan Buddhist's Wheel of Life—the idea that we all keep coming back until we get it right and lead virtuous enough lives that we finally earn our way into Nirvana.

Remember now, we're sixteen-year olds in high school. We know all about this stuff.

Monk wasn't sure he bought the Wheel of Life idea, but if it turned out to be true, if we did come back, he thought he'd like to come back as blue teapot.

So be on the lookout for him.

Monk liked the Rubaiyat.

There is a quatrain that fits:

Some we loved, the loveliest and the best
that rolling time hath from his vintage priest,
have drunk their little round or two before,
and one by one, crept silently to rest.

Rest easy, buddy."

Patsy

With Kathy and Kim and Meg on their way to something, probably church. Note the gloves. Chris hasn't made his appearance yet.

I Could Say...

I never thought in my wildest imaginings that I would wind up finding a way to make conversation to the same person for fifty years.

What in the world could you possibly find to talk about?

But we did, Patsy and I.

And are still at it.

On the occasion of our fiftieth wedding anniversary, a grand evening surrounded by family and friends on a hilltop overlooking San Francisco Bay, after the music and the wine, the laughing and the dancing, the time came for me to make the toast.

What do you say about a woman you've lived with and loved with, laughed with and fought with, put up with and been thankful for, since you were both just barely adults?

This is what was said then.

We're approaching our sixty-third as this is written and I may change a few of the words.

But not the sentiments.

"So here we are, fifty years later.

The highest satisfaction of these fifty years is our children, Kath and Meg and Kim and Chris.

They've turned out wonderfully. They are successful. They have good marriages and fine families. They meet their responsibilities and they don't abuse their advantages.

They are good people.

Patsy gets the credit for that.

I've had a reasonably successful career. Patsy should get most of the credit for that, too.

She took care of all the day-to-day stuff that has to be taken care of to make a home and raise a family while I was out running around enjoying myself in the corporate world.

I could say I love you.

But that goes without saying.

I could say I admire you—for what you've achieved—not only with the family, but with yourself.

I could note that once you'd gotten the kids up and out on their own, you went back to school to complete that undergraduate degree you were working on when we got married.

And then you went on to get a graduate degree in psychology. And with that you fashioned a successful career as a family therapist.

You are your own self-made woman.

I could say all those things.

Or I could say, simply …

Thank you.

So, friends, please raise your glasses and join me in a toast.

Patsy…

Thank you."

Déjà Vu All Over Again

The big night.

Graduation night for the Frankfort High School Class of 2017.

I've made the drive from Pinehurst up to Raleigh where the airport is, caught a Delta flight to Lexington, picked up a car, driven down to Donnie's in Frankfort, showered, shaved, made sure my white shirt is pristine, my tie knotted flawlessly, my navy blue suit unwrinkled, and am waiting in my place on stage as the graduates file in.

The auditorium is filled with parents and friends. All are relieved and excited and proud.

As am I.

It is no small thing to be invited back to make the graduation address at the school that launched you.

I'm introduced and stand to applause.

And savor it.

And remember back to my own graduation.

We assembled in the auditorium at the school on Shelby Street that night, less grand than here in the sparkle of the Convention Center, but friendlier, warmer, all sixty-three of us, capped and gowned, the girls never prettier, the boys never more well-behaved.

I remember.

And scan tonight's graduates sitting in rows in front of me and think, this is what the face of tomorrow looks like.

The big auditorium is still. I take a deep breath and begin.

"I haven't the foggiest idea of who the speaker was the night I graduated.

I remember the night well, but I have no clue of who he was or what he said. All I was interested in was getting that diploma, getting out of that cap and gown, and getting on with finding out what the night had in store.

I imagine that's your priority, too, and I understand and endorse it.

But there are a couple of points I want to cover that might be useful. I promise to make them without preaching, and as rapidly as possible.

They have to do with luck, and success, and working for a living.

Given the option of being good or being lucky, opt for luck. I have that on good authority. My own.

I've been very lucky in my career. Being born and growing up in this little town was among the best of it.

But luck is fickle. The lady cannot be counted on. So you have got to be good. Not rocket-scientist good. But competent good.

If luck smiles on you while you're in the throes of being competent, you'll be golden.

If you're good, though, really good, and she takes your hand—gang-busters.

You will all want to be successful, I imagine. The rewards of success are usually wealth and power and esteem. These are fine rewards, but they come at a price. The currency is determination, and discipline, very hard work ... and luck.

Some will not be able to pay the price.

They will not have been given the resources—physical, emotional, intellectual—that are required.

Some, even though they are able to, will not want to pay the price.

They'll conclude that they don't need to be Governor of the Planet Earth to be happy, and they'll go their own fortunate way, satisfied with who they are and with what they do and where they live.

A few, though—the ambitious, the gifted, the self-confident, those with remarkable self-discipline—they'll be eager to pay the price. They'll make their own luck, grab success, and lead us into tomorrow.

Regardless of the concerns, the idiocies, or the posturing of the times, this breed always has. For which we should be thankful.

I know you're hearing that the world is going to hell in a handbasket—bad vibes almost everywhere. But the mood of this June isn't all that different from the mood of that June when I graduated.

A week after our class got its diplomas, the Korean War erupted.

Then the Cold War exploded. People were planning fallout shelters that they hoped would protect themselves and their families when the atomic bombs started raining down. The economy was staggering. There were predictions that the End of Days was just around the corner. It seemed that might be true.

I raise this point because we made it from that *then* to this *now*, from *there* to *here*.

And it is better.

Every generation has made it better.

Yours will, too. We're counting on it.

One final comment.

When I graduated high school, my father said that his wish for me was that I would never have to work for a living. I liked that idea a lot. But since he wasn't a rich man and I knew of no relatives who were likely to leave me a fortune, I was confused.

It turned out that for him, working for a living was doing something you took no pride in, got no pleasure from.

Working for a living was having to do something you didn't like.

It could blister you, bruise you, bloody you, wear you out and drive you up a wall in frustration … but so long as you could see value in it … could take pride in it … get satisfaction from it … it wasn't working for a living.

By that definition, I have never had to work for a living.

My wish for you is that you never have to either.

Now I'm finished, and the night is yours."

III

CODA

There has been nothing about the visitors at Romance, yet.

Or what we did about the cyanide in the river.

Or the L.A. riots.

Or the Tech Center rapist.

Or the day they killed the King and brought the old King back.

Or Ghana.

Or the Holy Isle of Anglesey.

Or Trial by Television.

Or the search for that lost lane end into Heaven.

Even so, we've made it this far.

We have a story.

It has a beginning and a middle.

But no ending.

To get to that requires the part about the play of the game in the world of the steely-eyed executives and the god-like creatures.

Country boys and poets are strangers there,

More to come.

Author's Note

A bit of clarification about people.

Mom's maiden name is Clark. Patsy's is Schupp.

Ann's married name is Hatterick, Mary Lou's is Webb, Meg's is Muyskens, Kim's is Rhody (she kept her maiden name when she married Bob Burnett,) and Kathy's is Stewart.

I can't wrap this up without thanking Linda Hobson and Jane Snyder. Their editing made this a much better book than it started out to be. And Outer Banks publisher Anthony Policastro, whose personal involvement and attention to this effort enriched it.

And Darden Chambliss and Russ Hatter.

And Alice Irby and Edward Rofaxen Rogers.

And Donnie.

They read the early drafts and their reactions and suggestions helped me enormously as I tried to shape it into something worth publishing and decide whether to go forward with it.

I do thank them so very sincerely.

Which is not to say they were pushing me to get this into print. They felt that the matters hinted at in the prologue should be opened up and told about to complete the arc of the story.

And I intend to do that.

But not here.
This is about beginnings and becoming.
The rest of it has to do with the play of the game.
Those are different stories.

In the meantime, dear reader, my thanks for your time and kind indulgence.

Ron Rhody
Pinehurst, NC
June 28, 2018

The Author

Ron Rhody (Ronald E.) was a reporter, a sports writer, and a broadcast journalist before morphing into a career as a public relations executive. He spent most of his corporate career directing the public relations and advertising programs of two of the country's largest corporations. Later, he opened his own consultancy.

Now he is concentrating on writing and perfecting his drag-free drifts.

He and his wife Patsy live in Pinehurst, North Carolina.

ALSO BY RON RHODY

Fiction

The Theo Trilogy:
Theo's Story
Theo & The Mouthful of Ashes
When Theo Came Home

Concerning the Matter of the King of Craw

Nonfiction

The CEO's Playbook: Managing the Outside Forces That
Shape Success
Wordsmithing: The Art & Craft of Writing for Public
Relations
Soccer: A Spectator's Guide

PS: James B. and me

There's been enough about him in this story that you may be curious about what he looked like. He's a young man in his prime in this photo. He didn't get the chance to grow old. We're at a sportsman's club field day. That's a brand new double-barrel BB gun I'm being careless with. Got lectured about that. Never careless with a gun again. After that he put a fly rod in my hands. Thought it might fit me better, go better with my nature. It did. It does. Golden.